PUPPY PATROL™

JINGLE BELLE

BOOKS IN THE PUPPY PATROL™ SERIES

1. TEACHER'S PET
2. BIG BEN
3. ABANDONED!
4. DOUBLE TROUBLE
5. STAR PAWS
6. TUG OF LOVE
7. SAVING SKYE
8. TUFF'S LUCK
9. RED ALERT
10. THE GREAT ESCAPE
11. PERFECT PUPPY
12. SAM AND DELILAH
13. THE SEA DOG
14. PUPPY SCHOOL
15. A WINTER'S TALE
16. PUPPY LOVE
17. BEST OF FRIENDS
18. KING OF THE CASTLE
19. POSH PUP
20. CHARLIE'S CHOICE
21. THE PUPPY PROJECT
22. SUPERDOG!
23. SHERLOCK'S HOME
24. FOREVER SAM
25. MILLY'S TRIUMPH
26. THE SNOW DOG
27. BOOMERANG BOB
28. WILLOW'S WOODS
29. DOGNAPPED!
30. PUPPY POWER!
31. TWO'S COMPANY
32. DIGGER'S TREASURE
33. HOMEWARD BOUND
34. THE PUPPY EXPRESS
35. ORPHAN PUPPY
36. BARNEY'S RESCUE
37. LOST AND FOUND
38. TOP DOG!
39. STARS AND STRIPES
40. HUSKY HERO
41. TRICK OR TREAT?
42. LITTLE STAR
43. MURPHY'S MYSTERY
44. JAKE'S PROGRESS
45. JINGLE BELLE

JINGLE BELLE

JENNY DALE

Illustrations by Mick Reid
Cover illustration by Michael Rowe

AN
APPLE
PAPERBACK

SCHOLASTIC INC.
New York Toronto London Auckland Sydney
Mexico City New Delhi Hong Kong Buenos Aires

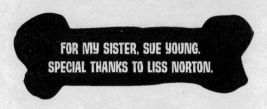

FOR MY SISTER, SUE YOUNG.
SPECIAL THANKS TO LISS NORTON.

ISBN 0-439-54366-5

Copyright © 2002 by Working Partners Limited.
Illustrations copyright © 2002 by Mick Reid.

Puppy Patrol is a registered trademark
of Working Partners Limited

All rights reserved. Published by Scholastic Inc., 557 Broadway,
New York, NY 10012, by arrangement with Macmillan Children's Books,
a division of Macmillan Publishers Ltd.

SCHOLASTIC and associated logos are trademarks and/or registered trademarks
of Scholastic Inc.

12 11 10 9 8 7 6 5 4   4 5 6 7 8/0

Printed in the U.S.A.
First Scholastic printing, November 2003

CHAPTER ONE

"**W**ow! Snow!" Neil Parker cheered. He stopped in the middle of the lane that led to the church and gazed up at the sky in delight. "We don't usually get snow this early in December."

His sister Emily held out her hands and caught some flakes on her gloves. "Do you think it will stick?"

"I hope so," Neil said with a grin. "I can't wait to go sledding in the park. And if it gets deep enough, maybe school will close early for Christmas." He bent down to pat Jake, his young Border collie. "Wouldn't that be cool, boy?"

Jake barked and licked Neil's hand.

"We'd better get a move on," said Emily. "I don't want to be late for rehearsal." She glanced at her

1

watch, tilting her wrist so that light from a nearby streetlamp shone onto it. It was almost seven o'clock. The Compton Amateur Dramatic Society, known as CADS for short, would be starting their play rehearsal in a few minutes. They were performing *Beauty and the Beast*, and Emily was playing one of the Beast's servants.

"Come on," she said, hurrying along the path that led through the churchyard. The church porch gates were standing open and, from inside, another door led to the church hall. Neil followed Emily inside with Jake at his heels.

The church hall was a long, low room with a stage at one end. Screens covered in black cloth stood on either side of the stage to create wings where the actors waited before their entrances. The hall was already full of people and, for some reason, everyone seemed to have brought their dogs with them! Mr. Hamley, Neil's principal, was striding backward and forward, going over his lines. His Dalmatian, Dotty, danced beside him. "Out, villain!" Mr. Hamley cried as Neil and Emily came in.

Emily giggled. "I think he means you, Neil."

"Maybe he thinks I should be at home doing my homework," Neil joked.

"It looks like Dotty wants to be in the play, too," remarked Emily.

"It's too bad she can't be. She'd bring the house down," Neil said, laughing. "She's so bouncy, she'd

probably literally bring it down by knocking over all
the scenery. Hey, Dotty!" The beautiful Dalmatian
bounded over to him and jumped up, planting her
front paws on his chest.

Mr. Hamley smiled briefly at Neil and Emily. "I
shall have my revenge!" he threatened.

Dotty jumped down and raced away across the
hall, barking excitedly.

"What part is Mr. Hamley playing?" Neil asked.

"Grim Jim, the baddie," said Emily. "Julie and I
have to pretend to be scared of him."

"I can't wait to see that!" Neil laughed again.

"I bet you could still be in the play, if you wanted
to," said Emily.

Neil shook his head firmly. "No, thanks. I'd rather
help out backstage." He looked around for Graham
Morris, the Parkers' next-door neighbor, who was
directing the play. Graham was perched on top of
a stepladder, fiddling with the wires of a spotlight.
Neil decided to offer his help later, when Graham
was less busy.

Alison Ford, a slightly built woman with long
blond hair, was laying costumes over chairs near the
back of the hall. She looked up and caught sight of
Emily. "Ah, Emily," she called. "I've got to measure
you for your costume."

"See you later, Neil," Emily said excitedly.

Neil looked around and spotted Holly, a young
chocolate-brown Labrador, on the far side of the hall.

Her owner, Alex Morgan, who was a friend of
Emily's, was kneeling beside her, rummaging through
a basket of costumes.

Jake trotted across to them, his tail wagging eagerly. Holly pricked up her ears as Jake approached,
then the two dogs touched noses.

Neil went over to join them. His parents, Bob and
Carole Parker, ran King Street Kennels, a boarding
kennel and rescue center in the village of Compton.
Neil had helped to look after Holly and her brothers
and sister when they'd been abandoned as tiny pup-
pies.

"Hi, Alex. Hello, Holly," he said, running a hand
over the Labrador's gleaming fur. Holly wagged her
tail and barked a greeting.

"Are you in the play, Neil?" asked Alex. She pulled
a silky pink dress out of the basket and smoothed it
flat.

"No way!" He caught sight of a pair of scarlet pan-
taloons in the costume basket and winced. Imagine
having to wear something like that!

Emily came over, carrying a pale blue dress. "Alison asked me to give you this, Alex. She thought it
looked about your size."

Alex took the dress, then held it and the pink one
up. "Which one do you think is better?" she asked.

"The blue one," said Emily.

"What do you think, Neil?"

Neil shrugged. Apart from the color, the dresses

looked identical to him. He heard a sniffing noise behind him and looked around. Jake had his head in
a basket of props. Neil whistled and Jake came
padding over with a silk flower dangling from his
collar.

"Jake must be trying to get a part in the play," Alex
observed, giggling.

Neil grinned, too. "Look at you," he teased. He
pulled the flower out of Jake's collar and put it back
in the basket.

The door opened and Julie Baker, Emily's best
friend, came into the hall. Ben, her enormous Old
English sheepdog, padded calmly beside her. "Hi,
everyone," said Julie. She stopped and looked around.
"I was hoping nobody would mind if I brought Ben

along with me, but I see everyone else had the same idea. Look at all these dogs! Did you learn all your lines, Emily?"

"Most of them," replied Emily. "I've been practicing a lot."

"I know Em's lines almost as well as she does," Neil joked.

"I'm struggling with mine," Alex admitted. "I was really happy when Graham picked me to be Belle, but now that I've seen how many lines I've got, I'm not sure I'll ever learn them all!" Alex was playing the lead in the play.

"You'll be fine," Emily reassured her. "You know your first three scenes already and you've only had the script for a few days."

Just then, Graham Morris came down from the stepladder and clapped his hands. Everyone turned to look at him. Even Dotty stopped capering about and sat down. "Thanks for coming, everyone. Can we try to run through scene four? The one where Belle comes to the Beast's castle?"

"That's us, Emily," said Julie. She thrust Ben's leash into Neil's hand. "Could you look after Ben for me while I'm doing my lines, please?"

"And Holly," added Alex. As she bent down to clip on Holly's leash, Dotty came bounding over. She danced around Holly, barking loudly, then pelted away across the hall. Holly and Jake darted after her.

"Holly, come back!" cried Alex.

"Here, Jake," Neil called. He held on tight to Ben's leash as the big dog tried to join in the chase.

Jake stopped and looked back at Neil. Then the Border collie trotted over to him and sat down. Neil took a dog treat out of the packet he always carried in his pocket and gave it to Jake. Then he gave one to Ben. "You're a good boy, too," he said, patting him.

"Holly!" Alex called as Holly and Dotty started sniffing at a large handbag that stood beside Mrs. Jepson's chair.

"Shoo!" cried Mrs. Jepson, flapping her hands. "Go away, you horrible dogs."

"Holly!" Alex called again. Holly looked around, then trotted back toward Alex.

Mr. Hamley strode after Dotty, red-faced with embarrassment. Dotty swerved away and cannonballed into a basket of costumes. The basket toppled onto its side. A heap of brightly colored clothes spilled out, and a pink silk scarf draped itself across the Dalmatian's back.

"Dotty!" Mr. Hamley growled sternly.

The naughty dog skidded to a halt and looked up at him, her mouth open wide in a doggy grin.

Mr. Hamley bent down and grabbed hold of her collar. Then he looked around at everyone. "Sorry about that," he said apologetically.

"Well, I'm glad I didn't bring Sugar and Spice!" Mrs. Jepson snipped. "They would have been terribly upset to see Dotty behaving so badly." Sugar and Spice were Mrs. Jepson's spoiled Westies.

Neil laughed, then hastily turned the laugh into a cough as Mrs. Jepson frowned at him. Mrs. Jepson's pampered pooches weren't exactly famous for their good behavior, either.

"Neil, since everyone seems to have insisted on bringing their dogs to rehearsal, I don't suppose you'd like to be the official CADS dog-sitter, would you?" asked Graham, coming over to retrieve the scarf from Dottie's back.

Neil grinned. "You bet I would."

"Excellent." Graham raised his voice. "OK, everyone. Neil's going to look after the dogs for us so we can get on with the rehearsal."

Neil started to shift some boxes of props to make room for his canine club. "Can you get me a bowl of water from the kitchen, Em?" he asked. "After all that excitement, the dogs are probably thirsty."

Emily nodded and ran off to find one.

"I'll get you a chair, Neil," offered Julie.

Neil cleared a space a couple of yards wide, to give the dogs plenty of room to lie down. Julie put a chair in the middle of it.

"Thanks," Neil said. He sat down and Jake and Ben flopped onto the floor beside him.

Alex brought Holly over. "I'm sure she'll behave herself now," she said.

"Of course she will," Neil agreed. "At least she's used up some energy!"

Emily came back with the bowl of water. "Here you are." She set it down, then glanced at the stage. "I'd better go. It looks like we're finally about to start."

"Thanks, Em," Neil said. "Good luck."

Jake and Ben watched the stage intently as Emily and Julie waited for Graham's signal to begin. Emily was holding a mop and Julie had a feather duster, so you could tell they were meant to be servants even though they weren't wearing their costumes.

Holly leaned comfortably against Neil's leg. Neil reached down and stroked her, remembering how tiny she'd been when he'd first seen her.

Mr. Hamley came over with Dotty walking calmly beside him. "This is very good of you, Neil," he said. He pushed Dotty's leash into Neil's hand and hurried behind one of the screens at the side of the stage.

At a signal from Graham, Emily began to mop the stage. "I love this time of year," she said brightly. "Everyone's so happy and —"

"Look out, here comes Grim Jim," warned Julie. She and Emily stepped back as Mr. Hamley marched onto the stage.

"Breakfast!" he demanded.

"I'll get it right away," said Emily, curtsying. She headed for the side of the stage, then stopped and looked around uncertainly.

"What happened to the knock?" called Graham.

"Sorry," Alex said, popping her head around the screen. "I was reading my lines. I'll do it now." She disappeared behind the screen again and knocked loudly.

"There's someone at the door," said Julie.

At that moment, the door of the church hall opened and a flurry of snowflakes blew in with a blast of cold air.

Emily began to giggle. "There really *is* someone at the door."

Gavin Thorpe, Compton's reverend, came in with his black Labrador, Jet. Neil thought he looked worried.

"People, I'm afraid I've got some bad news," Gavin announced loudly.

Everyone stopped to look at him.

"The church's insurance needs to be renewed," Gavin said, "and I had some safety inspectors in here this afternoon. They said that the whole place needs to be rewired."

A murmur of concern ran through the room.

"When will it be done?" asked Alison's husband Mark. "The play's in just a few weeks."

Gavin sighed. "That's the problem, I'm afraid. I'm trying to find an electrician to do the work quickly, but it's not looking too good, and we're not allowed to use the hall until the repairs have been completed. I'm really sorry, everyone."

Neil looked at Emily in dismay. Did that mean the play would have to be canceled? Around Neil, the dogs all stood up, as though they could sense their owners' anxiety.

"Oh, no!" Emily groaned.

"We can't give up now!" cried Julie.

"We've been working so hard at learning our lines and making props and costumes," said Alex.

Graham held up a hand for silence. "I'm sure this

is just a setback," he said. "We'll just have to find a
new venue for the play." He turned to Mr. Hamley.
"Paul, is there any chance we could use the school
auditorium?"

Mr. Hamley shook his head. "Sorry, Graham, it's
under construction."

"There's got to be somewhere else we can go," said
Alison.

Silence filled the hall as everyone racked their
brains to think of a new venue.

Neil felt bitterly disappointed. It wouldn't be fair
if the show had to be canceled — not after all the
work that everyone had put in. He ran his fingers
through Jake's fur and thought hard. There had to
be somewhere else it could be held.

Suddenly, Neil remembered the old village hall on
the other side of Compton. He'd gone to Cub Scout
meetings there years ago, but the troop met in the
church hall now and Neil wasn't sure that anybody
used the village hall anymore. It was a bit small, but
the audience wouldn't mind having to squish in.
"What about the old village hall?" he suggested out
loud.

"Where?" asked Graham, frowning. "I didn't know
there was a village hall in Compton."

"That's because you haven't lived here that long,"
Mrs. Jepson told him. "It isn't used much now."

"It's on the other side of Compton, down Purbeck

Lane," said Gavin. "It's not as big as this hall, but it would probably do."

"But what sort of condition will it be in?" demanded Mrs. Jepson. "The roof might have caved in or something."

"Alison and I walked past it the other day," said Mark Ford, "and it looked OK then. I think it's still used occasionally."

"My mom held a tag sale there a couple of months ago," put in Julie.

Neil patted Jake as he listened to the discussion. Jake licked his hand, then rolled over on his back so that Neil could scratch his tummy.

"I must admit, it does sound like a good idea. Thanks, Neil. I'll contact the council tomorrow and see if we can use it," said Graham.

"I bet they'll be glad to have something going on there," Alison pointed out. "After all, they still have to pay to maintain it."

"It's as good as ours, then," said Graham. He beamed at everyone. "The show *will* go on!"

CHAPTER TWO

"**I**'ll change the poster in the baker's," Neil said, "and you do the one in the supermarket." It was the day after the rehearsal, and he and Emily were on their way home from school. Neil had printed some bright yellow labels that said "OLD VILLAGE HALL," and he handed a sheet to Emily. "Here you go, Em."

While Emily went into the supermarket, Neil crossed the road to the bakery. Compton was already decorated for the holiday season with strings of lights looped across the road and a tall Christmas tree standing outside the post office. It was bitterly cold and there was a dusting of snow on the ground. Neil clapped his gloved hands together to warm them up, and wondered if they would get more snow in time for Christmas.

The baker's was looking festive, too. Gold and scarlet tinsel hung from the ceiling and there was an inflatable Santa Claus in the window.

"Excuse me," Neil said politely to the girl behind the counter. "I'm from the drama society. I need to change your play poster, please."

"Oh, OK," she said with a smile. "Help yourself."

Neil took down the poster and stuck a label over the old venue details. As he was replacing it in the window, an old man came along the road, walking briskly. He stopped to look in the bakery window, then his gaze fell on the poster and he frowned. He glared crossly at Neil before walking on.

Neil was puzzled. He couldn't see why anyone would be annoyed by a holiday play. He shrugged and went out of the bakery.

Emily was waiting for Neil on the other side of the road. "I hope the council will definitely say we can use the old village hall," she said. "Otherwise we'll have to change the posters again!"

"Graham seemed to think it would be OK," Neil said.

"Oh, no, he didn't!" Emily giggled.

"Oh, yes, he did," Neil countered, grinning. He glanced at his watch. "We don't have time to change any more posters now. We've got to go and pick up Nelson."

"Who?" asked Emily.

"Nelson. Dad asked us to get him on our way home from school," Neil reminded her.

Emily looked mystified. "He didn't ask *me* anything."

"Yes, he did," Neil insisted. "At breakfast this morning. Don't you remember?"

Emily shook her head. "I must have been reading my script. Who is Nelson, anyway?"

"Mrs. Trimble's dog. Mrs. Trimble's moving into The Grange because of her bad hip." The Grange was a retirement home in Compton.

"Oh, that's right," said Emily. "She asked Dad to find him a new home, didn't she?" She frowned. "Why can't Mrs. Trimble take him with her? After all, Flash lives at The Grange with Mr. Gilmour." Flash was a retired greyhound with a knack for retrieving things, which had proved very handy for the elderly residents.

"Mrs. Trimble can hardly walk," Neil explained, "so she won't be able to look after him properly."

"Poor Nelson," said Emily. "It'll be strange for him to have to leave his owner. We'll have to find him a really good new home."

"Yes, we will," Neil agreed. He thought about having to give up a much-loved dog and shivered. He wouldn't be able to bear it if he ever had to give up Jake.

Mrs. Trimble lived in a small house near the library. Neil rang the bell. A young woman wearing bright green overalls opened the door. "Have you come to take Nelson?" she asked.

"That's right," said Neil.

"I'm Sue, Mrs. Trimble's neighbor," the woman explained. "I'm helping her pack. She said she was expecting you." She ushered Neil and Emily inside, down a cheerful yellow hall and into the living room.

Mrs. Trimble was sitting in an armchair by her fireplace. She looked frail, but she smiled brightly when Neil and Emily came in. A walker stood beside her chair and there were lots of Christmas cards on the mantelpiece.

A big crossbreed dog lay on the hearth rug at Mrs. Trimble's feet. He had a short, smooth, white coat speckled here and there with black. On his back were two black patches and there was another one over his left eye. He looked up lazily as Neil and Emily came into the room.

"Hello," Neil said. "I'm Neil Parker and this is my sister, Emily."

"Hello, dear," said Mrs. Trimble. "Your dad said you would be coming."

Neil bent down to stroke the dog. Nelson looked at Neil trustingly before flopping over onto his side with a sigh of contentment.

"I'm so sorry you've got to give him up," said Emily.

Mrs. Trimble looked sad, but she managed to smile. "I know your father will make sure he goes to a good home," she said. "And there's no way I can take him with me when I move into The Grange."

"Why don't you two sit down for a minute and warm up?" Sue suggested. "You must be frozen."

"Thanks, but we have to get back," said Emily.

"Should we get Nelson's things?" Neil asked.

Mrs. Trimble pointed to a tote bag. "I packed his blanket and his food and water bowls. I put in a couple of cans of his favorite food, too. And there's his leash, hanging over the back of that chair."

Neil got the leash. The big dog lay still while Neil clipped it to his collar, then he pushed himself stiffly to his feet, his tail wagging. He had long legs and a rangy frame, but he didn't look much like any particular breed that Neil could think of. Neil stroked him thoughtfully. He loved *all* dogs, but even he had to admit that Nelson wasn't the best-looking dog he had ever seen.

"Come, Nelson," said Mrs. Trimble.

Neil let go of the leash and Nelson padded over to his owner. He rested his head on her lap and she rubbed the sides of his face. "Now, you be a good boy," Mrs. Trimble said quietly. She gave him a final pat, then held out the leash to Neil. "You won't have any trouble with him."

"I can see that," said Neil. "He's a great dog." He took the leash. "Come on, boy."

Nelson followed him trustingly across the room.

Emily picked up the tote bag. "I hope you like living at The Grange, Mrs. Trimble," she said.

"I'm sure I will," replied the old lady. "Please thank your father for looking after Nelson for me."

Neil could see that she was struggling not to cry.

Sue slipped a comforting arm around Mrs. Trimble's shoulders. "Off you go then," she said to Neil and Emily.

Neil glanced back at Mrs. Trimble as they went out of the room and gave her an encouraging smile. "He'll be fine," he promised. "We'll let you know how things work out."

"Do you think Nelson knows he's leaving her?" said Emily as they shut the front door behind them and set off down the street.

"Probably," Neil answered. "Dogs often sense their owners' emotions." He looked down at Nelson. "He's very gentle, but he's so big he'll need somewhere with a decent-sized yard. And there'll have to be enough room for him indoors, too. But I'm not sure he's young enough or lively enough for a family." Neil frowned. King Street Kennels had a great track record for finding new homes for dogs, but with Nelson he wasn't sure that it was going to be easy.

Bob Parker, Neil and Emily's dad, was coming out of Kennel Block One when Neil and Emily arrived home. "Hello, you two," he said. "Can you settle Nelson into the rescue center please, Neil?"

"Sure," Neil replied. "Are you coming, Em?"

"No, I've got to practice my lines. There's another rehearsal tomorrow evening." Emily handed over Nelson's tote bag and headed for the house.

"Come on then, boy," said Neil, leading the big dog into the rescue center. He spread Nelson's blanket out on his new bed. The dog sniffed it suspiciously, then ran to the gate of his pen, whining.

"You're staying here now," Neil told him. He pet Nelson until he quieted down, then brought him some dog biscuits and water. Nelson wolfed down the biscuits, wagging his tail. "At least you've got a good appetite," Neil remarked, grinning at the big dog. "Don't worry, boy. We'll find you a new owner soon."

Neil went to see Nelson before school the next day. He was lying curled up in his pen, but he lifted his head and looked at Neil, thumping his tail on the side of the basket.

"All right, boy?" Neil asked, going into the pen. Nelson's food bowl was empty — a good sign. The water bowl was empty, too. The rescue center heating was turned up because of the cold weather, making the place cozily warm, so Neil wasn't surprised that Nelson had drank all his water.

He refilled the water bowl, then grabbed a grooming brush. He waited while Nelson took a long drink before setting to work. Nelson stood quietly as Neil brushed him, looking around now and then as if to inspect Neil's handiwork.

At last, Neil stepped back to admire the dog. He still looked kind of funny, with his gangly legs, huge paws, and angular head, but his coat was smooth and clean. "You look great," Neil said approvingly.

Bev Mitchell, one of the kennel assistants, came into the rescue center. "Hello, Neil," she said. She put down the bag of biscuits she'd been carrying and came over to Nelson's pen. "You've done a fine job there," she said. "Nelson looks great now. I'm sure we'll find him a home soon."

Neil nodded as he smoothed Nelson's head. "I hope so," he said quietly. "He really deserves it."

CHAPTER THREE

The old village hall looked as if it was bursting at the seams when Neil, Emily, and Jake arrived the next evening. It was smaller than the church hall and the boxes of costumes took up so much floor space that there was hardly any room for the prop tables.

"My goodness, it's freezing out there," said a voice behind Neil.

He turned and saw Mrs. Jepson walking toward him with her two Westies, Sugar and Spice. They were dressed in matching Christmas outfits — tartan coats and a gold bow fastened to a topknot of hair between their ears. Mrs. Jepson was carrying two bulging bags.

"I'm glad you're here, Mrs. Jepson," said Alison.

"I've got a couple of costumes I'd like you to try on. They're in the dressing room behind the stage. Dr. Harvey's trying on his Beast outfit now, but there should be enough room for both of you." She glanced at Neil. "Would you mind keeping an eye on Bundle while I'm gone, Neil?"

Neil nodded. There was nothing he liked more than being left in charge of dogs. He bent down and stroked Alison's big, friendly mongrel. "What's up, boy?"

Mrs. Jepson put down her bags. "Dr. Harvey? But there are *two* dressing rooms, aren't there?" she asked.

Alison shook her head. "I'm afraid not. Everyone has to share."

Mrs. Jepson gave a shriek. "Share?"

"I'm sure we'll be able to rig up a curtain to split the room in half," said Alison quickly.

Mrs. Jepson looked horrified. "You can't expect *me* to change behind a curtain!"

"Don't worry," Alison reassured her. "It'll be a very thick curtain."

Sighing, Mrs. Jepson followed Alison backstage. Sugar and Spice trotted behind her.

Graham Morris arrived with Harry, his black-and-white cocker spaniel. "Are you up for some more dog-sitting, Neil?" he asked.

"You bet!"

"Great. Would you mind prompting, too, to help people if they forget their lines?" continued Graham. "We're working without scripts tonight."

"OK," Neil agreed. He took the script and flipped through it. It was a copy of the entire play and Neil knew he'd have to follow it closely.

"Come on, boys," he said to Jake, Harry, and Bundle. The three dogs pricked up their ears, then trotted behind him as he went up onto the stage for a closer look at the scene painting. Christine Holmes and Dan the builder were hard at work, painting the interior of a castle on an enormous board at the back of the stage. Dan was painting a sweeping staircase and Christine was putting the finishing touches on a grandfather clock.

"Did you bring Angel?" Neil asked Christine, looking around for her young West Highland cross. Angel's mom, Willow, belonged to Kate, the other kennel assistant at King Street.

"She looked so comfortable at home, curled up by the radiator, that I didn't have the heart to drag her out in the cold," said Christine, painting the last number on the clock's face.

"Can we get started, please?" called Graham.

Neil jumped down from the stage and found himself a chair. The dogs sat beside him, looking around curiously.

The door of the hall opened and Mr. Hamley came in with Dotty. "It just started to snow again," he said, taking off his gloves and rubbing his hands together. "And I'm afraid I couldn't find my script anywhere. I've got a horrible feeling that Dotty might have

eaten it. I found some suspicious scraps of paper behind the sofa this morning."

"We're not using scripts tonight," said Graham.

"Really?" Mr. Hamley looked anxious. "I'm not
sure that I'm ready . . ."

"Neil's prompting," Graham told him. "I'm sure
you'll be fine, Paul."

Mr. Hamley nodded, but he didn't look particu-
larly confident.

"Come on, Dotty," said Mr. Hamley. He led her
across to Neil. "I thought I should keep her on her
leash this evening. Would you mind looking after
her again?"

"Of course not," Neil said.

Mr. Hamley handed Neil the leash and Dotty
jumped up and licked his nose.

The rehearsal began. Emily and Julie came onstage carrying Alex's wedding veil and a bouquet of
silk roses. "I never thought I'd see the day when the
master would find himself a wife," said Emily.

"Nor me," said Julie. "And she's such a dear girl."

Alex hurried up the steps, wearing a long white
wedding dress. "The flowers are beautiful!" she cried,
taking them from Julie. She walked across the stage,
looking thoughtful and taking care to avoid the
paint cans.

Mr. Hamley was standing at the side of the stage,
waiting to go on. "Will there be screens or something

here, Graham?" he asked. "I'm supposed to give an evil laugh from the wings at this point, but the audience will see me if I stand here."

"Dan's going to make us some screens. The ones at the church hall were too big to move," replied Graham.

"Oh," said Mr. Hamley. Then he laughed wickedly, but before he could make his entrance, Mrs. Jepson swept out of the dressing room with Sugar and Spice at her heels. She was playing Belle's Aunt Esme. "May I interrupt?" she asked, holding her skirt up as she navigated her way around the paint pots and

down the steps. "I must just settle my babies before I go on."

She called to Sugar and Spice and they trotted down from the stage. Mrs. Jepson picked up her tote bags, then turned to Neil. "You will take good care of my poppets, won't you?" Without waiting for a reply, she opened the first bag. "Here's Spice's blanket." She took out a fluffy blue blanket and laid it on the floor, smoothing it out carefully. Then she lifted Spice onto it. "There you are, my little darling," she cooed.

Spice flopped down on the blanket, panting in his tartan coat.

"And this one's for darling Sugar," said Mrs. Jepson, taking a pink blanket out of the other bag. "We don't want you lying on the nasty cold floor, do we, sweetikins?"

Sugar stepped onto her blanket and lay down.

"Now, be good for Mommy," Mrs. Jepson said, stroking both of them.

Neil forced himself to keep a straight face. Mrs. Jepson was something else! There was no reason why Sugar and Spice couldn't lie on the floor. The other dogs didn't mind it.

"Let's get going, then," said Graham.

Mr. Hamley gave another evil laugh and strode forward. "So you think you're going to marry that beast!" he cried, catching Alex by the shoulders and turning her to face him. "You will . . . um . . ." He paused. "Sorry, Neil, I've forgotten the next line."

"You will marry me instead," prompted Neil.

Mr. Hamley repeated the line with a snarl.

Just then, the door to the village hall blew open and a little puppy scampered inside. She barked excitedly, then ran onto the stage, straight toward Mr. Hamley.

The teacher staggered back, tripping over an empty paint can. He lost his footing and fell against the wet backdrop with a cry of alarm.

Dotty jumped up, barking wildly. The sudden movement startled the black-and-tan pup. She leaped off the stage and raced across the hall.

"Quick, Em!" Neil cried. "Hold Dotty for me while I catch the puppy."

Emily jumped off the stage and ran to take the Dalmatian. Neil darted after the stray. She was sniffing around the costume boxes, giving little yaps of excitement. Neil stopped a few feet away from her. "Here, girl," he called in a low voice, trying to calm her.

The pup looked around, her eyes bright with mischief.

Neil moved slowly toward the little dog, knowing that a sudden movement might send her scampering away again.

"We'll give you a hand." Before Neil could stop them, people began to run toward the terrier cross. She watched them coming, ears cocked and tail wagging rapidly. Suddenly, she gave a high-pitched bark and dashed down the hall, diving between Graham's legs. Everyone raced after her.

"Wait!" Neil cried. "We need to move slowly."

Nobody was listening. They were all intent on catching the runaway dog, who obviously thought this was a great game. She charged up the steps and onto the stage again, knocking over a pot of gold paint. Neil watched, horrified, as the paint splashed over her fur and formed a wide gold puddle on the floor. The little mongrel ran through the puddle, leaving a trail of golden footprints behind her.

"Mind my poor babies!" shrieked Mrs. Jepson. "Don't let that stray near them."

The door opened and Miss Carter, the dance teacher, came in, followed by Neil's younger sister Sarah and the rest of her ballet class. They were taking part in the play, too. They stopped and stared in amazement when they saw the chaos.

"Here, girl," Neil called, sprinting toward the stage. The calm approach hadn't worked; he'd have to do something more drastic before the puppy wrecked the hall completely.

He pounded up the steps, but the puppy leaped off the front of the stage and dived under Alison's sewing table. As she came out on the other side, she bumped against a table leg. A pot of multicolored sequins tipped over and the glittering dots showered down on her.

Neil charged down the steps again. The runaway

pup looked as if she'd been decorated for Christmas. Her paws, her right ear, and most of her tail were covered in gold paint, and she was sprinkled with clusters of bright sequins that twinkled like stars. Not that she seemed to mind. She was barking with excitement and her tail wagged furiously.

"Come here, you," Neil muttered. He launched himself at the puppy once more, but the little dog was too quick. With a final, gleeful bark, she scampered down the hall, through Sarah's legs, and out the open door. By the time Neil got outside, she'd disappeared without a trace. He called and searched, but she'd vanished.

The actors gave Neil a round of applause when he reappeared in the hall.

"Where's the puppy, Neil?" asked Sarah. "Won't the paint hurt her?"

"It's harmless, it's nontoxic," called Dan from the stage.

"She'll be fine, Sarah," said Alison. "The paint will wash off. Just rolling in the snow will get rid of it. I wonder whose puppy it was. Hopefully they'll give her a bath when she gets home."

The discussion was interrupted by Mrs. Jepson. "I'm taking my babies away from this filthy mess." She glowered at Neil as she snatched up the blankets.

"What about the rehearsal?" Graham protested.

Mrs. Jepson didn't reply. She bundled the blankets into the tote bags, clipped on Sugar and Spice's leashes, and swept out of the hall.

"Oh, dear!" Alison sighed. "There's no way we'll be able to rehearse in here tonight."

Neil looked around. The puppy had left a trail of paint paw prints and sequins all over the place. The castle scenery had fallen down and there were costumes strewn everywhere.

"This play's doomed, if you ask me," muttered Dan. "First the church hall, now this."

"The play's not doomed," Graham said firmly. "We've had some bad luck, that's all."

"I'll take the dancers back to my house," said Miss Carter. "We can rehearse there. Line up, girls. And be careful not to step in any paint."

The dancers trooped out.

"Let's leave the paint to dry before we try to clean it up," suggested Mr. Hamley. "If we mop it now, we'll only spread it around."

There were murmurs of agreement. "Anyway, I doubt any of us feel in the mood for cleaning up at the moment," Christine added. "It seems to be one disaster after another."

Neil couldn't help agreeing with her. The play seemed to have been "dogged" by bad luck right from the start.

"So we'll call off tonight's rehearsal," said Graham. *He's trying to sound encouraging,* Neil thought, *but he looks really fed up.* "It won't take long to clean up tomorrow night, and then we can have a proper rehearsal."

"More work," Julie said with a sigh.

Neil pulled on his coat, whistled for Jake, and he and Emily headed for home.

CHAPTER FOUR

On Saturday morning, Neil was in Kennel Block One helping Bev feed the boarders when he heard a car coming up the driveway.

"I wonder who that is?" said Bev. "It's a bit early for the patients of Mike's clinic to come." Mike Turner, Compton's vet, ran a Saturday morning clinic at King Street Kennels.

"Let's hope it's someone looking for a dog," Neil replied. "It'd be great if we could find a home for Nelson before Christmas."

"Yes, it would," Bev agreed. "Especially since he's all alone in the rescue center."

Neil filled the last bowl, then hurried out to see who was there. Jake followed close behind. Mr.

Gilmour, one of the residents at The Grange, was getting out of his car.

"Hello," Neil called.

"Hello, Neil. Am I in time for the clinic?" asked Mr. Gilmour.

"Oh, yes," Neil said. "In fact, you're early."

Flash, Mr. Gilmour's retired greyhound, hopped awkwardly out of the backseat and limped toward Neil and Jake. Jake touched noses with the greyhound, then bounded away barking, as though inviting Flash to join in a game with him. Flash watched the young dog, but he didn't try to follow him.

"What's up with Flash?" Neil asked, concerned.

"He's not walking too well," said Mr. Gilmour. "That's why I brought him to see Mike."

"Do you think it has something to do with his missing toe?" Neil asked. The greyhound's toe had been amputated after a severe infection. The Parkers had found him dumped and injured by the roadside and had managed to save him, but not his toe.

"We'll have to see what Mike says," said Mr. Gilmour. He leaned into the car. "I'll come around and help you out, Jean."

Neil had been so interested in Flash that he hadn't noticed there was someone else in the car. Now he realized that Mrs. Trimble was with Mr. Gilmour. "Have you come to see Nelson, Mrs. Trimble?" he asked.

The elderly lady smiled up at him from the passenger seat. "Yes. Your father hasn't found him a
new home yet, has he?"

"Not yet," Neil said.

Mr. Gilmour lifted Mrs. Trimble's walker out of the
trunk and carried it around to the passenger door.
"Come on, Jean," he said, offering her his hand.

The old lady struggled out of the car, leaning heavily on Mr. Gilmour. "I'm so looking forward to seeing
Nelson," she said. "Has he settled in well?"

"He's fine," Neil replied. "He'll be really happy to
see you." He didn't want to worry Mrs. Trimble by
telling her how listless the big dog seemed.

"Flash and I will go to see Mike, then," said Mr.
Gilmour. "I'll come and find you when we're finished."

"This way, Mrs. Trimble," Neil said. He walked
slowly beside the elderly lady as she made her way
across the yard, leaning on her walker.

Jake charged across to them. "Steady, boy," Neil
said, placing a hand on the Border collie's head as he
skidded to a stop beside him.

After the biting wind outside, the rescue center
felt warm and snug. Sarah had draped tinsel across
the pens and there were sprigs of holly in a vase on
the counter where the dogs' food was prepared.

Nelson was drinking from his water bowl when
they came in, but he looked up and gave a joyful
bark when he heard Mrs. Trimble's voice.

"Nelson!" cried Mrs. Trimble.

"I'll get him out for you," Neil said. "Here, let me get you a chair." He fetched a chair and helped Mrs. Trimble to sit down. Then he ran to Nelson's pen.

Jake was already there, sitting near the door and watching Nelson with interest.

"Out you come, then," said Neil, going into the pen and clipping on Nelson's leash.

Nelson padded slowly beside Neil as they made their way out of the pen. "How are you, boy?" asked Mrs. Trimble as Nelson reached her.

He rested his head on her lap and she stroked his

face lovingly. The dog's tail wagged and he gave a single deep bark, as though to tell her how happy he was to see her. Neil was struck by his obvious affection for Mrs. Trimble. It was clear he'd make a perfect pet for a loving owner.

"He seems to be walking more slowly than before," said Mrs. Trimble.

"He does?" Neil asked. "Maybe he's feeling the cold. I'll put an extra blanket in his bed." He took one out of a cupboard and placed it in Nelson's basket.

"Has anyone been by to look at him yet?" asked Mrs. Trimble.

"Not yet," Neil admitted. "But I'm sure we'll find him a new home soon."

When Neil came out of Nelson's pen, Jake bounded up with a rubber ball in his mouth. He dropped it at Neil's feet.

Neil rolled the ball along the corridor that led to the outside door and Jake leaped after it. Nelson looked around, but he didn't join in the game. Instead, he flopped down on the ground with his head resting on Mrs. Trimble's feet.

"He used to like a game of catch," said Mrs. Trimble. She smiled. "I supposed he's just getting old, like me."

Jake seized the ball in his mouth and trotted back to Neil, but instead of dropping it so that Neil could throw it again, he lay down and started chewing it.

The door opened and Mr. Gilmour came into the

rescue center with Flash. "What did Mike say?" Neil asked, stroking the greyhound's ears.

"The poor old boy's got arthritis," said Mr. Gilmour. "Mike thinks it's because he's been walking awkwardly since his toe amputation." He sighed, then took a bottle of tablets out of his pocket. "He gave me some anti-inflammatory pills to reduce the swelling and help with the pain. And I've got to keep him moving as much as possible." He patted Flash. "So we'll be out for lots of walks, won't we, boy?"

"Poor Flash," Neil said. He knew arthritis could be very painful.

"We'd better get going," said Mr. Gilmour. "Are you ready, Jean?"

Mrs. Trimble gave Nelson a last pat and handed Neil his leash. Then Mr. Gilmour helped her to her feet.

"I hope Flash's pills work," Neil said. He smiled at Mrs. Trimble. "Please come and see Nelson whenever you want."

"Thank you, dear," she said. "And thank you for looking after him so well. I can see you've got a good way with dogs." Mr. Gilmour helped her to lift her walker into place, then she made her way slowly to the door. The two old people went outside with Flash limping behind them.

Nelson whined when the door closed, but he didn't resist as Neil led him back to his pen. "Good boy," Neil soothed as the dog settled down in his bed. He gave Nelson a dog treat and stroked him gently, then tucked his extra blanket around him to keep him warm.

The sky was heavy and gray when Neil and Jake came out of the rescue center again. Neil looked up hopefully, wishing for it to snow. Then he hurried into the house, eager to get out of the cold wind.

Emily was sitting on the floor by the stove, reading the *Compton News*. Sarah was sitting at the kitchen table. She was making a Santa Claus out of cardboard and cotton balls. "I'm going to stand this by Fudge's cage," she told Neil. "He likes Santa Claus." Fudge was Sarah's hamster and she thought he was the most intelligent hamster ever born.

Carole Parker came into the kitchen. "You look frozen, honey," she said. "Would you like some hot chocolate?"

"Yes, please," Neil replied. He started to tell his mom about Flash's arthritis.

"Look at this!" Emily interrupted. She sounded indignant. "Someone wrote a letter to complain about the play being performed in the old village hall."

"What?" Neil said, crouching down beside her to take a look. "Why would anyone complain about that?"

"He says the performers are blocking the lane with their cars," said Emily. "And listen to this part." She read aloud, "'There was a great deal of noise, both during and after the rehearsal.'"

"Well, we did probably make a bit of a racket when we were trying to catch that puppy," Neil admitted. "But it didn't go on for long. The letter's written by a councillor," he added, looking closer. "Jasper Longbridge. His address is on Purbeck Lane, too."

"I think he's got a lot of nerve," cried Emily. "I can't believe he wrote to the paper to complain about us."

"Well, he probably had gotten used to the hall being empty," said Carole, pouring hot milk into a mug for Neil. "It's usually very quiet down that lane.

Maybe he has a young baby who was disturbed by the noise. Or maybe his car was blocked in." She added some chocolate powder to the milk and handed the mug to Neil.

"Then he could have come and asked people to move their cars," Neil argued.

"And it's not as though a strange puppy is going to run riot at *every* rehearsal," Emily added. Suddenly, she stared at Neil in horror. "What if he stops us from using the hall?"

"He can't do that, can he?"

"He's a councillor," Emily pointed out. "And the council owns the old village hall."

Neil thought about all the work that had gone into the play so far. People had been learning their lines, painting scenery, and making costumes. They'd had lots of bad luck, but in spite of it all, they'd managed to keep the play going. What would happen if they lost *this* venue, too?

CHAPTER FIVE

Neil was eating his third slice of toast on Monday morning when the doorbell rang.

"Can someone get that?" Bob asked. He'd just come in from feeding the dogs and was pouring himself a cup of tea.

"I will," Neil said.

A tall lady, dressed in a fashionable coat and high-heeled shoes, stood on the step. "Good morning," she began as Neil opened the door. "My name's Mrs. Lloyd. I'm from the council. I'd like to speak to Graham Morris."

"Graham doesn't live here," Neil told her. "He lives next door, at Old Mill Farm."

Mrs. Lloyd frowned. "Oh, I'm sorry. Could you tell me how to get there, please?"

"I'll take you down there, if my parents say it's OK," Neil offered. "It's not far if we go across the fields, and I need to give my dog a run, anyway."

"Thank you. That's very kind of you," said Mrs. Lloyd.

Neil glanced at her expensive shoes. "It might be a bit muddy," he warned.

"That's all right, I've got some boots in the car," she said.

"Then I'll fetch Jake and see you outside," said Neil. He turned and went back into the kitchen.

"Who was it?" asked Bob, looking up from his cereal.

"Some woman named Mrs. Lloyd, looking for Graham Morris. She came here by mistake, so I said I'd show her the way across the fields." He whistled and Jake jumped up eagerly.

"I'll come with you," said Emily. "There's still half an hour before we have to go to school."

"Dress warmly," said Bob. "It's freezing out there. I think this wind's blowing straight from the Arctic!"

Mrs. Lloyd was waiting for them beside her car. She was wearing a pair of sturdy walking boots. They were worn and muddy and looked out of place with her trendy skirt.

"It's this way," said Emily, heading around the side of the house. They crossed the yard and went through a gate to the footpath that ran to Old Mill Farm.

Neil wondered why Mrs. Lloyd had come. It must

have been something urgent for her to arrive so early in the day.

"You live in a lovely part of Compton," said Mrs. Lloyd, looking around. "It must be a sight to see in summer."

"It's kind of windy at this time of year, though," said Emily, wincing as a fierce gust hit them. "You'll have to get a ride to school, Neil. You'll never be able to bike in this."

It didn't take long to reach Old Mill Farm. They hurried around to the front door and rang the bell. Neil rubbed his frozen cheeks, trying to get some feeling back into them.

Jo Morris opened the door. "Hello," she said, clearly surprised to see them so early. "Is everything all right?"

"This is Mrs. Lloyd. She's here to see Graham," Neil explained. "She came to our house by mistake."

Graham appeared at the end of the hall. "Did I hear my name?" he asked.

"Are you Graham Morris?" asked Mrs. Lloyd.

"That's right." Graham came down the hall, looking puzzled.

"I'm here from the council," said Mrs. Lloyd. "We've had some complaints about noise and parking at the old village hall. I'm afraid the council has decided that you can't use the hall for the CADS play after all."

"What?" cried Emily.

Neil stared at Mrs. Lloyd in disbelief. "That noise the other night was just a one time thing," he began. "One of the dogs got a bit excited and —"

"I'm sorry," Mrs. Lloyd interrupted, "but the council's decision is final."

"Now, wait a minute," said Graham. "The council gave us permission to use that hall."

"Well, the councillors have changed their minds," Mrs. Lloyd told him. "I'm sorry, Mr. Morris, but I'm afraid you'll have to find another venue for the play."

"How can we?" Emily burst out. She was red-faced with anger. "We can't use the church hall or the school auditorium. There's nowhere else in Compton."

"People have worked hard for this show," said Jo Morris. "If they can't use the hall, the holiday play will have to be canceled."

"There's been a play in Compton every Christmas for years," added Neil. "It's tradition."

"That doesn't change anything," said Mrs. Lloyd. "The council has to take all the town residents' feelings into account."

"Mr. Longbridge is behind this, isn't he?" Emily said furiously. "I saw his letter in the paper."

"I really can't say," said Mrs. Lloyd. "Now I must be going." She opened the door.

"What about our props and costumes?" asked Graham.

"They must be moved out of the hall this evening," said Mrs. Lloyd. "Thanks for bringing me over, Neil and Emily. I can find my own way back. And I really hope you manage to find another venue. Good-bye." She went out, shutting the door behind her.

"This is terrible!" Emily groaned. "What are we going to do?"

There was a gloomy silence. Jake padded across to Neil and pushed his wet nose into Neil's hand.

"There's not much we *can* do," Graham said at last. "The play will have to be canceled."

"It's so unfair," Emily complained. "I can't believe there won't be a play this year."

Neil glanced at his watch. "Hey, We'd better get a move on or we'll be late for school! Come on, Em." He

whistled for Jake and they left hurriedly, calling
their good-byes.

"We'll have to find somewhere else for the play,"
Neil puffed as they jogged back across the field.
"Maybe Gavin will manage to find some electricians
to rewire the church hall before Christmas. Then the
play can be performed there."

"But what about rehearsals?" said Emily. "We
can't put on a show that we haven't practiced!"

Neil fell silent. Emily was right. Even if the
church hall rewiring *was* completed sooner than expected, CADS couldn't perform the play if they hadn't
been able to rehearse it beforehand. He watched
Jake bounding along the path ahead while he tried
to come up with a solution. Surely there had to be
somewhere in Compton that was big enough for rehearsals?

Suddenly, Neil thought of the perfect place. "I've
got it! CADS can use Red's Barn!"

Emily's eyes shone. "That's a brilliant idea! It's
definitely big enough."

"Dad's dog training classes are already on hiatus
for the holidays, so it's free all the time at the moment," Neil went on.

Emily began to run faster. "Let's go and ask Mom
and Dad about it now," she shouted.

"It sounds like a good idea to me," said Bob, when
Neil had told him his plan. "Although we don't want

people wandering into the kennel. They might disturb the dogs."

"Everyone will be too busy rehearsing for that," Neil pointed out.

Bob nodded. "That's true."

"Hold on a minute," said Carole. "We'd better check with Bev before we make a decision. We use Red's Barn for exercising the dogs when it's wet, don't forget, so it'll be awkward for her if it's full of play props and backdrops."

"She won't mind," said Emily, grabbing her homework from the kitchen table and stuffing it into her bag.

"And what if Gavin doesn't manage to get the church hall rewired in time?" continued Carole. "It will be even worse if the play has to be canceled at the last minute."

"We don't *want* to cancel it, though," said Emily. "Everyone's really determined that it go ahead."

Carole laughed. "All right. I can see I'm not going to get a minute's peace until I say yes."

"That's settled then," said Bob. "We'll have a word with Bev, and if she's happy with the idea, I'll stop by Graham's later and let him know. Now let's get you two to school or you'll both be late."

A copy of the *Compton News* was being passed around when Neil, Emily, and Bob arrived at the old village hall that evening.

"Have you seen the letter in the paper about the play?" asked Alex, running over to meet them.

Neil was about to reply when Mr. Hamley spoke. "At least the paint paw prints have dried, so we can get on with rehearsing." He beamed at everyone. "I think things are going to be much better from now on."

"That's right," agreed Alison Ford.

Neil and Emily exchanged glances. The group obviously didn't know about the latest setback.

Just then, Graham arrived, looking serious. Without taking off his coat, he called everyone over. "I'm afraid I've got some more bad news," he said. "We're not going to be able to use this hall after all."

There were gasps of dismay.

"But it's OK, folks," Graham went on quickly, holding up his hands. "Bob and Carole Parker have agreed to let us use their barn for rehearsals. And we'll just have to hope that the church hall is rewired in time for the performance."

"I told you this play was doomed," said Dan.

"It's been one thing after another," complained Mrs. Jepson, sinking dramatically into a chair.

"But Red's Barn is a good place for rehearsals," Alex pointed out. "It's really big."

"And the Parkers won't complain if we're noisy," added Julie, smiling at Neil.

"If we don't take up their offer, we'll have to cancel the show altogether," Graham said firmly. "And I'm sure none of us wants to do that."

Everyone agreed that the show had to go on, but the cheerful mood had evaporated.

"We need to get all this stuff packed up," Graham continued. "Then we can transport it to Red's Barn."

Alison Ford began to fold up the costumes and put them into crates. "Here, I'll give you a hand," Emily offered.

"So will I," said Alex, collecting some feather-trimmed hats that were piled on a table.

Dan positioned a stepladder in front of the background scenery. "Can you help me dismantle this, Neil?" he called.

Neil hurried over.

"It's made up of six different boards, so it will fit in my pickup truck. Could you hold it halfway down, so it doesn't topple over?"

At first there was a general air of gloom in the hall, but gradually, as the props and lights were packed away, spirits lifted. "That didn't take long at all," remarked Mr. Hamley, dragging a heavy plaster statue toward the door.

"And it shouldn't take long to unload when we get to the Parkers'," Alison pointed out.

Dan finished unscrewing the first board and Neil took it out to his truck. It was surprisingly light. There was already a line of people waiting to load things into the King Street Kennels' Range Rover.

The hall was completely empty by the time Dan and Neil took down the last two backboards. When they carried them out to Dan's truck, the cast members were getting into their cars for the short drive to King Street Kennels.

Mark Ford leaned out of the window of his car. "See you at Red's Barn, everyone," he called.

Mr. Hamley tooted his horn and gave him a cheerful wave.

"The show must go on," trilled Mrs. Jepson as she climbed into Mr. Hamley's passenger seat.

Bob wound down the window of the Range Rover. "I don't have room for you and Emily, Neil, but Graham's going to give you a ride."

"OK," said Neil.

One by one, the cars drove away. "I bet Mr. Longbridge won't like all this noise, either," said Neil. "He'll probably write another letter to the paper about us."

It only took five minutes to reach King Street, and the boxes and crates were already being unloaded when Graham pulled into the driveway. Neil and Emily started emptying Graham's car trunk while Jake and Harry charged off to play with Bundle.

Mark Ford staggered past with a pair of heavy gold chairs. "The barn's great," he puffed enthusiastically.

Neil and Emily lifted a crate of props out of the

trunk. "We'll have to carry this together," Emily said between gasps. "It weighs a ton!" They lugged it between them into Red's Barn.

"Well, it's certainly big enough," said Mrs. Jepson, looking around the barn as she came in with Alison's sewing box. "But where are we supposed to change into our costumes? There isn't even a curtain in here!"

"We'll rig something up soon, Mrs. Jepson," promised Mark Ford. "Is it OK to move these straw bales,

Bob? I thought we could build a kind of changing room out of them."

"Sure, I'll give you a hand," Bob replied.

"I'll help, too," offered Neil. He followed his dad and Mark down to the end of the barn.

Eventually, Red's Barn started to look like a real performance venue. Alex, Emily, and Christine had almost finished laying planks on the floor at the far end to mark out an area for the stage. The scenery boards were propped against the wall behind the planks, and Mrs. Jepson and Julie were arranging props on a table.

The boxes of costumes were lined up in front of the straw-bale changing area and Alison kneeled beside them to take out red tunics and black pants. "Can I have all the soldiers over here for a fitting, please?" she called, raising her voice to make herself heard above the noise the dogs in the boarding kennel had suddenly started to make.

"Sorry about the racket," Neil said with a rueful grin. "The dogs will quiet down in a while. They always bark when we get visitors."

The six soldiers hurried over to her.

"Has anyone seen the soldiers' hats?" Alison called.

"I'll look for them." Neil began to rummage through one of the boxes.

Carole Parker came into the barn carrying a tray of drinks and small sandwiches. "Refreshments, anyone?" she asked.

Graham and Mr. Hamley helped themselves gratefully. "You're a lifesaver," said Graham, taking a sip from his mug. "This is just what we need." He raised his voice. "Places, everyone! Can we get ready for scene five, please?"

As the actors went to their marks, Neil found the box containing the soldiers' hats. He passed it to Alison, then picked up the prompt script and found a seat on a straw bale near the stage area. He whistled for the dogs, who were working their way around the barn with their noses to the ground. They padded happily across to him. "Sit," he commanded.

Jake and Ben sat down at once, their tails sweeping the floor. Harry and Bundle looked around longingly, as though they wanted to continue exploring. "Sit," Neil said again. They flopped down and he gave each of them a couple of dog treats.

He looked around for Dotty, but there was no sign of her. For a moment Neil felt worried. Perhaps she was still running around outside on her own. Then Mr. Hamley came over to him. "I left Dotty home tonight," he whispered. "Between you and me, I think Graham was getting fed up with her."

One by one, the boarders stopped barking. Soon the barn fell into a busy silence. The soldiers were trying on their costumes and Alison was pinning up sagging pant hems. Mark Ford was unpacking a crate containing the props that would be needed for scene six. The actors on stage smiled encouragingly at each other as they waited for Graham's signal to begin.

Neil felt a sudden surge of hope. In spite of all the bad luck, it looked like the play might go on after all.

CHAPTER SIX

"**L**ast day of school tomorrow," Neil declared cheerfully as he and Emily wrapped Christmas presents at the kitchen table. It was Tuesday afternoon and Bob was busy in the kennel, settling in a new boarder. Carole and Sarah had gone shopping.

"I can't wait," said Emily. She wrote out a gift tag and stuck it to a present.

Neil cut a piece of wrapping paper to fit the bubble bath he'd bought for his mom. Before he could start to wrap the bottle, he heard a car pull up.

"I hope that's not Mom and Sarah," cried Emily, jumping up.

The doorbell rang.

"It can't be Mom. She'd come in the back way,"

Neil said. "It's probably someone who wants to board their dog over the holidays." He glanced at the clock. "Mom could be back at any minute, though, so maybe we should put away the presents now."

"You get the door and I'll hide everything," said Emily.

Neil went to the front door. On the step stood an old man wearing a beige raincoat. Neil recognized him. It was the man who'd frowned at him when he'd changed the venue on the poster at the baker's. "Hello," Neil said. "Do you want to book your dog into the kennel?"

"No. My name's Mr. Longbridge and I've come about . . ." The man gestured toward his car, which was parked in the driveway.

"Mr. Longbridge?" Neil echoed. He'd heard that name before. "The councillor?" he asked.

The man looked puzzled. "That's right."

Neil's heart sank. It was Mr. Longbridge who had written to the paper complaining about CADS using the old village hall. He must have found out that they were rehearsing in Red's Barn and come to complain about that, too. Neil couldn't understand why he was so opposed to the play going forward.

"I believe you take in stray dogs," said Mr. Longbridge hesitantly.

Neil nodded warily. Was Mr. Longbridge going to object to *that* as well?

"I hope you'll be able to find room for a puppy," the

old man continued. "I found her in the lane that runs past my house."

"A puppy!" Neil felt himself smiling with relief. "Where is she?"

"In my car."

Neil followed Mr. Longbridge to the car and peered through the window. Curled up on the backseat was a tiny terrier cross with a short black-and-tan coat. It was the puppy who had caused chaos at the play rehearsal!

Mr. Longbridge unlocked the car and opened the back door.

The puppy lifted her head and looked up at them. She had a pretty face, soft, pointed ears, and deep brown eyes. Neil guessed that she was probably six or seven weeks old. Moving slowly so as not to frighten her, he reached into the car. The puppy leaned forward to sniff his hand, then licked him with a rough pink tongue.

"Good girl," Neil murmured, fondling her ears.

The puppy stood up and padded along the seat toward Neil. He lifted her out of the car and held her in the crook of his arm. She was so thin that she hardly weighed anything. Her fur was muddy in places, but there was no sign of any gold paint. Neil didn't think she'd been living outdoors for long; such a young puppy wouldn't have been able to feed herself in the wild. Angrily, he realized that she'd probably been dumped.

Bob came around the side of the house, blowing into his hands. "I thought I heard a car," he said. "What have you got there, Neil?"

"A lost puppy," Neil said. "Mr. Longbridge brought her in." He figured it was best not to tell his dad where he'd seen her before, in case the councillor started complaining about the play.

"Where did you find her?" asked Bob, turning to the old man.

"In the lane that runs by my house," Mr. Longbridge explained. "I hung on to her for a couple of hours, in case she'd just wandered away from her owners, but nobody seemed to be looking for her."

Jake appeared at the side gate and trotted over to sniff the new arrival.

"What a fine dog!" said Mr. Longbridge.

Neil felt himself warming to the old man. "Should I put the puppy in the rescue center, Dad?" he asked.

"Yes, thanks, Neil," said Bob.

Mr. Longbridge reached out and stroked the puppy. "Good-bye then, girl," he said gently.

"You can come and help me settle her in if you want," Neil told him.

The old man smiled. "Thank you. I'd like that very much indeed."

"And I'll give Sergeant Moorhead a call," said Bob. "Just in case somebody's reported a missing pup."

"We could call Mike Turner, too," Neil suggested. "He might know where she came from. And if he doesn't, we could get him to check her over and give her vaccination shots." He looked around for Jake. He was bounding through the courtyard, so Neil left him to play.

Nelson was lying in his basket when Neil and Mr. Longbridge went into the rescue center. The big dog lifted his head and looked at them, but he didn't get up.

"That's a good-looking dog," remarked Mr. Long-bridge. "He's got a little English pointer in him, by the look of it." He walked over to Nelson's pen and bent down somewhat stiffly to look at him through the wire.

Neil looked at Nelson. He was certainly big enough to be a pointer cross, and he had black speckles on his white coat, just like an English pointer. "I think you're right," Neil said, impressed.

"I used to own a pointer," Mr. Longbridge explained. "He was a wonderful dog — very loyal and intelligent."

Neil smiled. Even if Mr. Longbridge didn't like plays, he obviously loved dogs.

Neil carried the puppy into the pen next to Nelson's and laid her in the basket. Then he gave her a quick checkup, to make sure she had no obvious injuries. She seemed perfectly healthy, and squirmed impatiently until he let her jump out of the bed.

"You stay here and I'll get you something to eat and drink," Neil said. The puppy darted in front of him, almost tripping him up as he headed for the door of the pen. Neil picked her up and carried her back to her bed again. "Stay," he said firmly.

The puppy jumped out at once and pounced on Neil's sneakers. Laughing, Neil held her back as he went out of the pen. He shut the door behind him and filled a small bowl with special puppy food. Then he filled a second bowl with water and took them to the little dog. She squirmed around his feet, yapping with excitement. Her tiny tail wagged furiously.

"There doesn't seem to be much wrong with her!" Neil chuckled as he slipped out of the pen for the second time. The puppy was digging into the food, her tail still wagging.

Mr. Longbridge reached through the mesh of Nelson's pen and stroked the big dog with one finger. "It's funny how much you miss a dog," he said thoughtfully. "Caesar, my pointer, died a month ago, but I still think about him every day. The house seems so empty without him."

"Have you thought about getting another dog?" Neil asked hopefully. Perhaps Mr. Longbridge would want to adopt Nelson or the puppy.

"I could never replace Caesar." Mr. Longbridge sounded very firm as he straightened up and headed for the door. "Thank you for taking care of the puppy. I hope you find her a good home."

As Neil followed Mr. Longbridge outside, he wondered if the old man would be on his own for Christmas. Maybe he would like to come to King Street for Christmas dinner? Neil would be able to talk to him about pointers then.

Before he could ask Mr. Longbridge about his plans, Carole pulled into the driveway. She stopped the car and climbed out. "Hello," she called.

Sarah jumped down from the backseat, holding a box of Christmas cookies. "Look what we bought, Neil," she cried. "They're special cookies with china animals inside. I hope I get a hamster in mine." She

danced across the yard. "And we've got a box of cup-
cakes and some chocolates and Mom ordered the
turkey, too."

"What a waste of money," muttered Mr. Longbridge. "Christmas is much too commercial, if you
ask me."

Neil breathed a sigh of relief. Thank goodness he
hadn't said anything to Mr. Longbridge about Christmas dinner. He might know a lot about pointers, but
he didn't sound like he'd be much fun to have around
on Christmas Day!

Carole came over to shake hands with the councillor. "Hello. Have you come to choose a dog?" she
asked.

"Mr. Longbridge found a lost puppy," Neil explained.

"A puppy!" Sarah exclaimed, dropping the cookies
and dashing to the door of the rescue center. "Can I
see it?"

"If you want to," said Carole, picking up the box of
cookies. "You go with her, Neil. I'll get Emily to give
me a hand carrying in the shopping bags." She
smiled at Mr. Longbridge. "It was kind of you to go to
the trouble of bringing the puppy to us."

"Oh, it was no problem. I'll be on my way then."
Mr. Longbridge nodded briskly and walked back to
his car.

Neil followed Sarah into the rescue center. The

puppy was looking out through the mesh of her pen with her head to one side.

"She's the puppy from the play rehearsal!" Sarah gasped. "She's so sweet!"

Neil unlocked the pen and Sarah hurried inside. "Go slowly," Neil warned. "You don't want to frighten her."

He didn't have to worry about that. The puppy raced over to Sarah, barking a greeting, and jumped onto her foot.

"Can I give her a name?" Sarah asked excitedly.

"OK," Neil replied.

"I'm going to call her Belle, like Alex in the play, and like Jingle Bell for Christmas." Sarah stroked the tiny pup. "Do you like your new name, Belle?"

The puppy gave a high-pitched bark. "She does," exclaimed Sarah. She sat down beside the puppy. "Here, Belle. Good girl."

Belle climbed onto Sarah's lap, then tried to scramble up her chest to reach her face.

Sarah giggled. "She really likes me."

Nelson stood up and padded across to the mesh that separated his pen from Belle's. He watched the puppy with interest.

"Bring Belle to see Nelson," Neil suggested.

Sarah eased the puppy off her lap and stood up. "Here, Belle," she called, patting her leg as she walked across the pen.

Belle scurried after her. She spotted Nelson and scampered up to the wire with her head tilted back so she could look up at her long-legged neighbor.

Nelson lowered his head and the two dogs sniffed each other through the mesh.

"They're making friends!" Sarah squealed.

The door of the rescue center opened and a gust of icy wind blew in.

Mike Turner came inside, stamping his feet. "My goodness, it's cold out there!"

"You got here fast," Neil said in astonishment.

"I was just leaving to visit a sick cat when your

dad called, so I thought I'd stop in here on my way. Where's this puppy?"

"Here," said Sarah. "She's called Belle. I chose her name."

Mike came into the pen. "It suits her perfectly," he said. "She's a real beauty." He opened his bag, took out a stethoscope, and listened to the puppy's heart and lungs.

"She seems perfectly healthy." He took a needle from his bag. "I'll just give her a shot so she doesn't catch any nasty doggy diseases."

Neil held on to Belle while Mike did his work, but the puppy lay still in his arms, completely unconcerned. "You don't know of any litters like her around here, do you?" Neil asked.

Mike shook his head. "No. She's got no collar, and she's a cross-breed, which might mean she wasn't an expected pup. I'm afraid that she's probably been dumped." He closed his bag. "Still, I seriously doubt you'll have much trouble finding her a home. She's a real cutie pie. How's Nelson doing, by the way?"

"He seems fine," Neil told him. He placed Belle in Sarah's arms and the puppy snuggled up to her happily. Neil smiled. With Sarah spoiling her and Nelson keeping an eye on her from the pen next door, it looked like Belle would be very happy in the rescue center until they found her a new home.

CHAPTER SEVEN

"**H**as anyone seen Sarah?" asked Carole, coming into the living room on Wednesday evening.

"Isn't she in her room?" said Neil. He was helping his dad hang gold and red streamers across the ceiling. "She was being really secretive earlier," he added. "I thought maybe she had gone up there to wrap our presents."

"No, she didn't," Carole said, frowning. "It's not like Sarah to be slow getting ready on ballet night."

"Especially now that she's practicing for the play," Emily agreed, looking up from a box of Christmas tree decorations.

Neil jumped down from the arm of the couch. "I'll go and see if she's in the rescue center with Belle."

"Good idea," said Bob. "She's certainly crazy about that little pup."

Jake trotted after Neil as he went into the kitchen. "No, boy, you stay here," Neil said. "You can come with me to rehearsal later."

It was cold and dark outside and frost was already forming on the ground. Neil grinned. Today had been the last day of school. It would be perfect if it snowed now so that he could go sledding and have snowball fights with his friends.

He went into the rescue center. Sarah was sitting on the floor in Belle's pen. She was cradling the puppy in her arms and talking to her in a low voice.

"Come on, Squirt. It's time for ballet," said Neil, going into the pen.

Sarah made a face. "I want to stay with Belle. She gets lonely by herself."

"She's got Nelson to keep her company," Neil said. The big dog was lying beside the mesh that divided his pen from Belle's, watching the puppy.

"But she wants me," Sarah pouted.

"So does Mom," Neil told her.

Sarah lifted Belle into her basket and covered her with the blanket. "Stay here, Belle," she whispered. "I'll come and see you again later."

Neil felt a pang of sympathy for Sarah. She seemed to be growing really fond of Belle, and he knew it would be heartbreaking for her when they

found the puppy a new home. He bent down and ruf-
fled Belle's ears. *She is very cute,* he thought, as she
twisted her head around and licked the inside of his
wrist. It would be heartbreaking for all of them to
see her go.

Before they knew it, it was opening night. The
church hall was still being rewired, so Bob and Carole had agreed that the show could be held in Red's
Barn. For the previous two days, everybody who
could had helped to get the barn ready. Chairs for
the audience had been brought from the school, decorations had been put up everywhere, and Dan had
worked hard to finish the stage.

Now the barn was bursting at its seams. Members
of the cast milled about in colorful costumes, chat-
tering excitedly behind the curtain. "You look beautiful, Alex," cried Emily as her friend appeared
wearing her costume.

Mark and Alison Ford walked past with the cardboard sleigh that Alex was going to ride in on to her
wedding.

Graham's spaniel Harry began to growl. "It's OK,
boy," Neil said, laughing. "It's only a sleigh."

Mark and Alison stopped and let Harry sniff the
sleigh so he could see that there was nothing to be
afraid of.

The little girls in Sarah's ballet class were standing at one side of the barn dressed as snowflakes, in

white tunics and tights dotted with silver sequins. Neil noticed that Sarah was missing. He guessed she must have gone indoors for something.

"Places please, everyone," called Graham.

The audience settled into their seats, gazing at the curtain, waiting for it to rise. Behind it, Mr. Hamley glowered at the people around him, obviously getting into character, ready for the start of his scene. Mrs. Jepson smoothed down her dress and patted her hair into place. Mark Ford switched on a tape recorder and cheerful music began to play.

"Ready, girls?" asked Sarah's dance teacher when the actors were in position. "Where's Sarah?" she added.

"I'm here," Sarah called from the edge of the stage. She ran to her place in the line. The dancers skipped onto the stage and stood with their arms raised, ready to start their dance. The curtain rose, the music changed, and the dancers began to twirl in time to it, like snowflakes drifting in the wind.

Suddenly, Neil heard a jingling noise. He looked around, but couldn't see where it was coming from. The jingling grew louder. Mrs. Jepson glared at Neil, evidently thinking that he was to blame. Beside him, Jake pricked up his ears.

The dance ended and the snowflakes fluttered to the back of the stage. Now that the music had ended, the jingling seemed louder than ever. Neil turned around again. What in the world was going on?

"What *is* that noise?" whispered Bob, who was sitting beside him.

Suddenly, Belle ran onto the stage, her tail wagging. A line of tiny silver bells was draped around her neck, jingling musically with every step. The audience laughed and cheered. Sarah, Neil noticed, was looking very guilty.

"Oh, no!" exclaimed Bob. "Sarah must have smuggled Belle backstage."

Belle looked around, her brown eyes full of mischief, then ran straight for Sarah. The actors onstage looked at one another, not sure what to do.

Then Alex stepped forward and saved the day. "Where has my little puppy gone?" she asked.

As if on cue, Emily, her servant, replied, "I think she's out playing in the snow."

The audience laughed, the actors smiled in relief, and the show went on.

At the interval, Graham marched over. "Really, Sarah," he said. "We've had enough problems without 'jingle dogs.'"

Sarah hung her head. "Sorry," she said. "But Belle wanted to watch me dance."

The puppy squirmed around in Sarah's arms and licked Graham's hand.

Graham smiled, though Neil could see he was trying to look stern. "Well, I think we'll have to keep her in the show now. She's a star. The audience loves her."

Everybody enthusiastically agreed. The puppy obviously loved being the center of attention, and she wasn't at all bothered by the lights or the costumes.

"You'll have to look after her when she's not onstage, though, Sarah."

"I will," Sarah promised, hugging Belle tightly.

The rest of the show went really well and Belle behaved beautifully. Neil watched her trotting beside Alex as she moved across the stage. The puppy seemed to know instinctively where she had to be at all times. When the play ended and the actors came forward to bow, Belle got a standing ovation.

"Bravo, everyone," called Graham. "And bravo, Belle. You've definitely got star quality!"

"Let's go and put Belle back in the rescue center, Sarah," said Neil, as people began to make their way out to their cars.

"I wish I could keep her forever," Sarah said sadly, rubbing her cheek against Belle's head. "She's the best dog ever!" She glanced at Jake. "Well, as good as Jake, anyway."

"We'll find her a really great home," Neil told her gently.

Sarah sighed. "I know. But I love Belle, Neil. I love her as much as Fudge."

"I know you do, Squirt," said Neil. He was going to miss Belle, too, when they found a home for her. He hoped her new family would live nearby, so that they'd still be able to see her now and then.

The next day was the first day of school vacation. Neil jumped out of bed even earlier than usual, thinking how much easier it was to get up when he *didn't* have to go to school. He helped Bev feed the boarders, then went looking for Emily. "Let's take Jake and Belle to The Grange," he suggested. "I'd like to see how Flash is doing."

"OK," agreed Emily. "Sarah's gone with Dad to buy the Christmas tree, so she won't miss Belle while we're out."

It was a ten-minute walk to The Grange and Belle trotted beside Jake all the way, looking around eagerly, as though she didn't want to miss anything.

They passed through The Grange's ornate wrought-iron gates and set off up the tree-lined driveway. Ahead of them, in front of the house, stood a tall Christmas tree decorated with colored lights. "I can't wait for Christmas!" Neil said with a grin.

They were halfway to the house when a minibus overtook them. It pulled up beside the front steps.

"There's Mr. Gilmour and Flash," said Emily as the old man came out of the front door with the greyhound limping beside him.

"Poor Flash," said Neil. "He doesn't look much better."

"How was your swimming trip?" called Mr. Gilmour as some of The Grange's residents climbed out of the minibus.

"Wonderful!" replied a lady in a bright green tracksuit. "It's done wonders for my stiff old joints. Watch this." She bent down and touched her toes.

"Bravo!" cried Mr. Gilmour. He caught sight of Neil and Emily. "Hello, you two."

"We came to see how Flash's arthritis is," Neil said, crouching down to stroke the greyhound.

Mr. Gilmour shook his head as he patted Jake and Belle. "Not too good, I'm afraid."

Suddenly, Emily gasped.

"What's up?" asked Neil.

She shrugged. "Nothing. I just had an idea, that's all."

"What sort of idea?"

Emily smiled mysteriously. "I'm not saying. I might be wrong."

Neil was intrigued. "What might you be wrong about?"

"Wait and see," said Emily. "I'll tell you when we get home."

"Here it is!" cried Emily, bursting into the living room. "I knew I'd seen it somewhere!"

Neil was sitting by the fire. He looked up from his book. "What?"

"An article about hydrotherapy in one of my dog magazines." Emily held the magazine out to Neil and he saw a photo of a golden Labrador paddling energetically in a small swimming pool. "It's a way for dogs with arthritis to exercise without putting weight on their sore joints," Emily explained.

Neil took the magazine and skimmed the article quickly. "So you think it might work for Flash?" he asked.

"Yes," replied Emily. "It's basically just swimming, and that lady at The Grange said swimming had helped her."

Bob had come in from the kitchen. "This sounds interesting," he said. "I wonder what Mike Turner thinks about hydrotherapy for dogs. Why don't you give him a call and find out, Neil?"

Neil ran to the phone and dialed Mike's number.

"Well, it's certainly worth a try," said Mike when Neil had told him Emily's idea. "Flash is really suffering at the moment, and I've heard it can work wonders with racehorses."

"Thanks, Mike. Bye." Neil hung up. "Let's e-mail the hydrotherapy center and ask if Flash can come to their pool," he said to Emily. He stuck his head into the kitchen where Carole and Sarah were making some mince pies. The room smelled deliciously spicy.

"Can Emily and I send an e-mail, please?" Neil

asked. He noticed that a batch of mince pies was already cooling on a wire tray. "Would you like me to try one of those for you, just to make sure they're OK?"

Carole laughed. "Go ahead. But only one, or we won't have enough for Christmas. And take one for Emily."

Neil took the mince pies and he and Emily went into the office and switched on the computer. They ate their mince pies while they waited for it to connect to the Internet. "I hope they'll let Flash use their pool," Neil said, brushing pastry crumbs off the desk. "I'm really worried about him." He glanced at the magazine article again and crossed his fingers for luck. The hydrotherapy pool looked exactly like what Flash needed.

CHAPTER EIGHT

"**A**re you sure you don't want to come Christmas shopping with us, Neil?" Carole asked on Friday morning.

"No, thanks," Neil replied. "I'm going tomorrow afternoon with Chris. I think I might take Jake out to the park. Would it be OK to take Nelson, too?"

"Sure," said Bob. "It'll do him good to have a long run."

"See you later then," said Carole. "Come on, Bob. We'd better get going or we won't be able to park."

"Can Belle come with us?" asked Sarah.

"No, she can't," Carole replied firmly. "She'd hate trailing around the stores. She'll be much happier in her nice, warm pen."

"I'm going to buy her a present," Sarah announced. "And one for Fudge, too."

Bob, Carole, Sarah, and Emily pulled on their coats and trooped out to the Range Rover. Neil put his coat on, too, then he whistled for Jake and went out to fetch Nelson. The sun was shining, the sky was bright blue, and the bitter north wind had eased up.

Nelson was standing by his water bowl when Neil went into the rescue center. "Come on, boy. We're going for a walk," Neil said, clipping on Nelson's leash.

Belle was curled up in her basket. She looked up sleepily as Neil led Nelson past her pen, and gave a little bark as though she were saying good-bye.

Nelson barked back, then followed Neil outside.

Bev was crossing the yard with a can of dog food in one hand. "I was just coming to feed Nelson," she said. "I gave him some of that new food this morning, but he didn't like it. I've got a different type here that he might like more."

"If you leave it in the rescue center, I'll feed him when I get back," Neil promised. "We're going out to the park now."

Neil kept Nelson on his leash as they set off up the steep path that led to the park. Jake pranced around them, sometimes running ahead, sometimes darting away to sniff at interesting scents in the bushes.

Nelson seemed to find the climb hard. Now and

then he flopped down for a rest, panting. Neil decided to ask his dad if Nelson could have some extra exercise to improve his health.

They reached the top and Neil let Nelson off the leash. Jake still had lots of energy left. He charged backward and forward, bounding over clumps of tall grass and veering around bushes. Nelson plodded along behind him, stopping now and then to sniff the ground.

Neil strode after them. He loved being up in the park. Compton was so far below them that it looked like a model village. Windows glittered in the winter sunshine and smoke curled up from the chimneys.

All at once, Jake gave a warning bark. Neil turned to see what was wrong.

Jake was standing stock-still, his ears drooping and his tail tucked between his legs. He was gazing at something on the ground, but Neil couldn't see what it was because it was obscured by long grass.

"What is it, boy?" Neil called. As he ran forward, he saw what had upset Jake. "Nelson!" he yelled.

The big dog was lying motionless on the ground. Neil threw himself down beside Nelson and touched his side gently. Nelson didn't respond. Panic-stricken, Neil felt the dog's chest. His heart was still beating, but he was unconscious.

"Stay with him, Jake," Neil commanded. He leaped up and raced away along the top of the hill.

Soon he reached a path that led out to the road. Glancing back, he saw that Jake was still standing guard over Nelson.

Neil ran along the path, his heart pounding so hard he thought it would burst. As he reached the road, he saw a car coming. "Help!" Neil yelled. Ignoring his own safety, he ran into the road, waving his arms.

The car skidded to a halt.

Neil ran to the driver's door. "Help! My dog collapsed," he gasped. "I've got to get him to the vet."

To Neil's total astonishment, the driver was Mr. Longbridge. "Where is he?" he demanded, unbuckling his seat belt and opening the door.

"This way," Neil said, racing back the way he'd come.

Mr. Longbridge hurried after him, moving surprisingly quickly for an elderly man.

The black-and-white dog hadn't moved. Neil's hand was shaking violently as he felt for Nelson's heartbeat again. To his intense relief, the dog's heart was still beating and, when Neil looked closer, he could see his chest rising and falling with quick, shallow breaths.

Jake whimpered and nudged Nelson with his nose.

"It'll be all right, boy," Neil promised. "Mike'll make him better."

"It's that pointer cross, isn't it?" panted Mr. Longbridge. "What happened to him?"

"He just collapsed," Neil told him. He took off his coat and spread it out on the ground. "If we can get him onto my coat it'll be easier to carry him."

"Good idea," said Mr. Longbridge.

They gently maneuvered Nelson onto the coat, then lifted it carefully. Neil felt as though his knees would buckle under Nelson's weight as they made their way slowly to the car. Jake walked quietly beside them, his brown eyes looking worried.

They reached the car at last and laid Nelson on the hood while Mr. Longbridge opened the back door.

Kneeling beside Nelson, Neil stroked the dog's coat. "Hang on, boy," he begged. He rested his hand on Nelson's head and willed him to wake up.

The dog didn't move.

"Let's get him in," said Mr. Longbridge.

They hoisted Nelson onto the backseat, adjusting

his legs so that he was lying comfortably. The big white head lolled on his paws, making Neil's stomach clench with worry. Jake jumped in, not taking his eyes off the motionless shape.

Neil climbed into the front seat. Mr. Longbridge started the engine and they sped away down the road toward Compton.

Mike Turner was just getting out of his car when they arrived at his clinic.

Neil leaped out as soon as Mr. Longbridge's car stopped. "Help, Mike!" he yelled. "Nelson collapsed."

Mike ran to see. "Let's get him inside," he said. He helped Mr. Longbridge carry the dog into the clinic and lay him on the examining table. "Tell me exactly what happened."

"I took Nelson and Jake up to the park," Neil explained. "He just fell over."

"Did he seem tired at all?" prompted the vet.

"Yes, especially when we got to the top."

"Did he eat this morning?" Mike asked.

"Bev said he didn't eat his breakfast," Neil told him. "I was going to give him some food when we got back."

Mike lifted Nelson's eyelids and examined his eyes. "Has he been drinking a lot?"

Neil nodded. "Yes, he has. Why? Do you know what's wrong with him?"

"It could be diabetes, but I think we've caught it in

time. If he hasn't eaten today, his blood sugar level will be too low. I'll put him on a glucose drip. That should help."

Neil watched as Mike got a bag of liquid glucose. He couldn't help feeling guilty for not realizing how ill Nelson was. He should have seen that something was wrong.

"Don't look so worried, Neil," said Mike after he'd set up the drip. He patted Neil's shoulder. "Nelson will be fine."

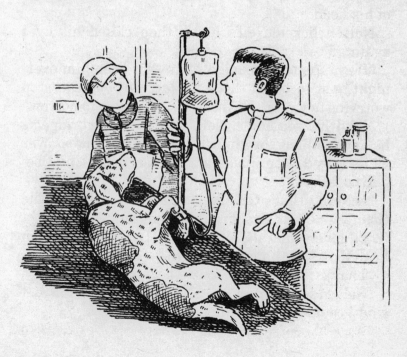

"I've read something about diabetes in dogs," said Mr. Longbridge. "It's relatively easy to control it through diet, I believe."

"Yes, it is, as long as it's in the early stages," Mike agreed. "Nelson's food will need to be monitored very carefully from now on to make sure he doesn't have another attack like this one."

Suddenly, Nelson opened his eyes.

"He's awake!" Neil cried. He bent over Nelson, overjoyed to see him conscious, and stroked the side of his head.

Nelson licked Neil's hand, then closed his eyes again.

"He needs to rest," said Mike. "I'll keep him overnight, just to be on the safe side. But you can stop worrying now, Neil. He'll be as good as new tomorrow."

"I'll drive you home, Neil," said Mr. Longbridge as he and Neil left the clinic. The sky had clouded over while they'd been inside and a light drizzle had begun to fall.

"Actually, that's OK," Neil said. "I should go to The Grange and tell Mrs. Trimble what happened."

"I'll give you a lift," offered Mr. Longbridge. "Then I can drive you home afterward."

"Thanks," Neil said. "You've been really kind."

"Nelson's a fine dog," said Mr. Longbridge. "I'm just glad I could do something to help him."

*   *   *

Mrs. Trimble was chatting to Mr. Gilmour in the greenhouse when Neil and Mr. Longbridge arrived at The Grange. Flash was lying at Mr. Gilmour's feet.

"Hello, Neil," called Mr. Gilmour as they went in.

Jake trotted across to Flash. The greyhound lifted his head to sniff Jake, but he didn't stand up.

Neil quickly told Mrs. Trimble about Nelson's diabetes. "Mike Turner says he's going to be fine," he finished.

"Poor Nelson," said Mrs. Trimble. "I didn't realize there was anything wrong with him. He had been getting a bit slower recently, but he's not the only one!"

"He's a good dog," said Mr. Longbridge warmly. "I used to have an English pointer, you know, and Nelson reminds me of him. You shouldn't worry too much about the diabetes. I understand it can be controlled with his diet as this stage."

"How's Flash?" asked Neil.

"Not too good," said Mr. Gilmour, reaching down to stroke his dog's velvety ears. "Those pills haven't made a lot of difference, I'm afraid."

Neil told Mr. Gilmour about Emily's hydrotherapy idea. "But they might not be able to fit him in," he finished cautiously. "We haven't gotten a reply to our e-mail yet."

"It sounds as though it'd do him a world of good!"

Mr. Gilmour declared. "I just hope Flash gets the chance to go there."

"Me, too," Neil agreed. He stood up and whistled for Jake. "I'd better get home. Mom and Dad will be wondering what happened to me."

He went across to Mr. Longbridge. He and Mrs. Trimble were deep in conversation. "You have family in Canada?" Mr. Longbridge was saying. "My daughter and son-in-law live there, too, near Vancouver." He sighed. "I miss them, especially at this time of year." He glanced over at Neil. "Are you ready to go?"

"Don't worry, Mr. Longbridge, I can walk from here," Neil said. "It's not far. Thanks very much for all your help."

As he went out of the greenhouse, he glanced back. The three elderly people were deep in conversation, and Mr. Longbridge looked more relaxed than Neil had ever seen him.

The rest of the Parkers were still out Christmas shopping when Neil got home. He made a mental note to remind his dad to call Mike about Nelson as soon as he got in. Then, with Jake padding at his heels, he went into the office and switched on the computer. There was one e-mail waiting for him.

Dear Neil,

Thank you for your inquiry concerning our hydrotherapy pool. Due to a cancellation, we have a space in our schedule for 11:30 a.m. on Monday, December 23. Please confirm as soon as possible that you will be able to attend at this time.

"Yes," Neil shouted in delight. He punched the air. "See that, Jake?" he said. "Flash is going swimming!"

CHAPTER NINE

"**M**orning, Neil," said Carole cheerfully when Neil went downstairs the next morning. She was making more mince pies — they'd already eaten the first batch.

Emily was sitting at the kitchen table, frowning over her lines for the play. Sarah sat beside her, finishing a slice of toast.

Bob came in from the yard while Neil was pouring himself a glass of orange juice. His face was red from the cold.

"I'm going to go see Belle," Sarah announced, getting down from the table and grabbing her boots.

Neil saw his parents exchange a worried glance. "Why don't you go later?" Bob suggested. "You could finish Fudge's cardboard Santa Claus."

"I finished it yesterday. And Belle's waiting for me," Sarah said firmly as she went out.

"Is Belle all right?" Neil asked.

"Of course she is," his mom replied. She began to spoon mincemeat into the rounds of pastry.

"Would anyone like some toast?" Bob asked.

"Yes, please," Neil said. "You are *sure* that Belle's all right?"

"Yes," said Bob, sounding a bit agitated. He put bread into the toaster. "One slice or two?"

"Two, please," said Neil. Just then he heard a car pull into the driveway. "That's probably Mike," he said. "I wonder how Nelson's doing." He jumped up and hurried outside.

Nelson was sitting in the back of Mike's car, looking out of the window. His eyes were bright and his ears were pricked up. Neil felt a rush of relief to see him looking so well. "Is he OK?" he called.

"He's much better," said Mike, climbing out of the car. "Are your mom and dad around? I need to talk to them about his new diet."

"They're in the kitchen. Go right in." He opened the car door and Nelson jumped out. "Come on, boy." Neil caught his collar and led him to the rescue center.

Sarah was there already, playing with Belle. The puppy was bounding around her pen in pursuit of a rubber ball.

"Has she been fed, Squirt?" Neil asked.

"Bev fed her," Sarah told him. She clapped her hands delightedly as Belle dropped the ball at her feet. "She's so smart. She's already learned to fetch a ball."

Neil took Nelson to his pen and the big dog ran straight to the wire that divided him from Belle. She scampered over to greet him, her tail wagging.

Bob came in. He looked at Nelson and smiled. "He responded well to that glucose treatment. He looks energetic."

"So does Belle," said Sarah.

Bob sighed. "You're spending a lot of time with Belle, Sarah. You know she'll be going to a new home one day soon, don't you?"

Tears sprang into Sarah's eyes. "But why can't *we* keep her? I love her most of all," she whispered.

"I know," said Bob. He went into Belle's pen and put his arms around Sarah. "But we can't keep all the dogs who come in here. There'd be no room for us in the house if we did that."

So that's why they looked so worried, Neil thought. They'd noticed how fond Sarah was getting of Belle and they didn't want her to be upset when the puppy found a new home.

"I don't want all the dogs!" Sarah said with a sob. "I just want Belle."

Neil's heart went out to her. Poor Sarah! She'd really fallen for Belle.

"Perhaps you should spend a little less time with her," Bob suggested gently.

Sarah cried harder than ever. "No. I want to be with Belle all the time."

Belle ran to Sarah and sat at her feet, whining.

Sarah pulled away from Bob. She picked up the puppy and cuddled her. "Belle wants to be *my* dog," she muttered.

"You know we have to let the dogs go when we find good homes for them," Bob reminded her. He reached out for Sarah again, but she pulled away from him and turned her back, burying her face in Belle's fur.

CHAPTER TEN

"**C**ome on, Neil!" Bob called up the stairs. "We don't want Flash to be late for his hydrotherapy appointment."

Neil grabbed his swimsuit and a towel and bundled them into a duffel bag. He wasn't sure that he'd be allowed to go into the water with Flash, but it couldn't hurt to be prepared.

Emily and Bob were waiting in the hall when Neil came downstairs. Jake watched hopefully as Neil grabbed his coat.

"Not you, Jake. You stay here," Neil said. "We're taking Flash swimming."

Mr. Gilmour was waiting for them on the steps of The Grange. Flash sat beside him, his ears drooping, but he perked up a little when Neil opened the door of the Range Rover and called to him. The greyhound limped slowly to the car and Neil lifted him in. Mr. Gilmour climbed into the front seat.

"Liverpool, here we come!" cried Emily as Bob drove away.

"I hope Flash has been practicing his breaststroke," Bob joked.

Mr. Gilmour laughed. "He's been practicing his back crawl, too."

Unusually, so close to Christmas, there wasn't much traffic, and just over an hour after they'd left Compton, Bob turned into the parking garage of a modern, single-story building. "Here we are," he said.

The hydrotherapy pool was a raised tank about five feet wide by ten feet long. A ramp led up to it, and there was another leading down into the water. A digital sign on the wall showed that the water temperature was 82 degrees Fahrenheit.

Lisa, the therapist, fitted a buoyancy aid around Flash's body. "That's so you don't sink, boy," she said, giving him a reassuring pat.

Flash stood with his tail down, trembling.

"It'll be all right, Flash," Neil said, smoothing his ears. "You'll enjoy it."

"Greyhounds aren't big fans of water," Lisa warned, "but once he's in, he'll be fine." She grabbed a long pole and fastened it to Flash's buoyancy aid.

"What's that for?" asked Neil.

Lisa pointed at the water. "There are two water jets in the pool," she said. "The dogs need to swim in the jets so that they get enough exercise. I can guide Flash into the jets with the pole."

Neil could see the water bubbling gently just below the surface of the pool.

"The jets are adjustable," continued Lisa. "They're set on low for Flash, because he's never been here before, but, as he gets better at swimming, I'll adjust them."

"Is he ready to go in now?" asked Emily.

"Yup." Lisa guided Flash up the ramp. When he reached the top, he stopped dead in his tracks. "In you go, Flash," she coaxed.

Flash refused to move, and his lip curled in a growl when Lisa gave him a gentle push. He seemed absolutely determined not to budge an inch.

"What are we going to do?" Mr. Gilmour asked anxiously.

"Well, it's not standard procedure for people to go into the pool, but I think it might be the only way to get Flash in," said Lisa, frowning.

"I'll do it," Neil offered eagerly.

"Good for you," said Mr. Gilmour. "I'm not sure I'm up to splashing around in the water!"

Neil was soon changed. He scrambled over the side and into the pool, which was much warmer than a normal swimming pool. The bubbles tickled as they surged around his legs. The water reached up to his waist at the end where Flash was. He waded over to the ramp. "Come on, Flash," he called.

The greyhound looked at him with mournful eyes.

"Good boy," said Neil, reaching out to him.

Flash sniffed his wet fingers, then took an unsteady step down the ramp so that his front paws were in the water.

"Atta boy," Neil said encouragingly.

Flash took another step, then another. Soon he was halfway down the ramp and the water was up to his chest.

"We'll have him swimming any minute now," said Lisa. "Move farther out, Neil, and let's see if he'll follow you."

Neil stepped back. "Come on, boy," he called.

Suddenly, Flash launched himself forward. A moment later he was swimming, with his nose held high and his paws paddling the water. "Good boy!" cried Neil.

Using the pole, Lisa steered Flash into a water jet. The greyhound paddled harder and Neil could see that he was enjoying himself. His dark eyes shone with pleasure.

"This is excellent," said Lisa. "He's really working those muscles, and his aches and pains will be much less because the water is bearing his weight."

"He looks like a new dog!" admitted Mr. Gilmour.

Neil stayed in the pool with Flash for nearly half an hour. They swam up and down, side by side, through the water jets, while Lisa called encouragement from above.

"That's long enough," said Lisa at last. "We don't want Flash overdoing it."

Neil swam to the ramp. "Come on, Flash," he called.

Flash stayed in the middle of the pool.

"Look at that," said Emily. "He must have enjoyed it, because he doesn't want to get out."

Neil swam back to get him. "Come on, boy," he said. He guided Flash to the ramp and watched as he walked up out of the water. To Neil's delight, the elderly dog seemed to be moving more easily already.

"I think it's done him some good," he said. "This was a great idea of yours, Em!"

"He should show some improvement every time he comes," said Lisa as she ushered Neil into the locker room. "Not to mention your swimming, of course!" she teased. "To benefit the most, though, he should come weekly."

Mr. Gilmour looked glum. "That might be difficult. I don't drive, and I don't know how we can get here regularly. I can't ask the Parkers to bring us."

Bob sighed. "I'm afraid it would be impossible for us, as much as I'd like to help. But we'll think about it and maybe we can come up with a solution."

"We should have a hydrotherapy pool at King Street Kennels," Neil declared on the way home. Flash was lying on the seat beside him with his head on Neil's lap. He was fast asleep, and Neil guessed he was probably worn out after his swim.

In the rearview mirror, Neil saw Bob's eyebrows shoot up. Then his dad laughed. "Oh, Neil! You and your ideas!"

"Does that mean you wouldn't want one?" Neil asked.

Bob laughed again. "Well, it would be a great idea if we had the space, the money to install it, and the time to run it."

Neil was just about to offer to run it himself when he saw a snowflake float past the window. "It's snowing!" he shouted. He pressed his nose to the glass and gazed up at the leaden sky. More snowflakes drifted down.

"We're going to have a white Christmas after all!" Emily cheered.

When they got back to The Grange, Mr. Longbridge was there waiting for them. Mr. Gilmour had told him about Flash's arthritis and he was eager to find out if the hydrotherapy pool had helped. He was delighted to hear how successful it had been.

As the Parkers turned to leave, he came after them. Surprisingly, he wanted to apologize for having stopped the play from being held in the old village hall. "I'm so sorry," he explained awkwardly. "I felt so sad about being alone for Christmas that I couldn't stand to think of everybody else having so much fun. I behaved like a real Christmas scrooge."

Neil glanced at his father. He knew they were thinking the same thing, and he smiled when Bob told Mr. Longbridge it was OK, then invited him to the Parkers' for Christmas dinner.

Mr. Longbridge's face lit up. "That's extremely kind of you," he said. "Although I'm afraid I'll only be able to come at lunchtime. Mrs. Trimble has asked me to join her at The Grange in the evening for carols and a Christmas feast." He smiled at Neil. "It looks like I'll have lots of company this year!"

*   *   *

Mr. Longbridge came early on Christmas, bringing with him the biggest box of chocolates Neil had ever seen. It had been snowing heavily ever since they'd gotten back from the hydrotherapy center two days before, and Mr. Longbridge had to stamp the snow off his boots before he came inside.

"You didn't have to bring anything," said Carole, showing him into the living room. "We're just glad to have you here."

"And I'm glad to *be* here," replied Mr. Longbridge. "I hope it's all right," he added. "I've brought bones for Nelson and Belle. I know Nelson's on a special diet for his diabetes. . . ."

"A bone won't upset his diet," Carole reassured him.

"I was just going out to the rescue center to see Nelson and Belle," Neil said. "Do you want to come and give them the bones yourself?"

"I'd love to," said Mr. Longbridge.

Neil whistled and Jake jumped up from his place by the fire. He was wearing a bright red Christmas bow around his neck. "How about we go see Belle and Nelson, boy?" Neil said.

Jake barked, then followed Neil as he and Mr. Longbridge went outside. Snow marked with trails of footprints lay thickly on the ground. Jake threw himself down and rolled over, sending up a shower of loose flakes.

"You silly dog!" Neil laughed. He reached out to brush the snow from Jake's coat, but Jake darted away, barking excitedly. Snow had been blown into drifts along the north wall of the rescue center. Jake bounded over and buried his head in one. He emerged, sneezing, with a snow-covered face.

"You've got a fine dog there," said Mr. Longbridge.

Neil felt a rush of pride. He loved it when people praised Jake. "Thanks," he said as he opened the door to the rescue center.

Nelson and Belle were lying on either side of the wire mesh between their pens.

"Hello there, Nelson," said Mr. Longbridge, walking toward him. "And hello, Belle. Aren't you growing?"

Neil opened Nelson's pen and Mr. Longbridge went inside. He unwrapped the bone and held it out to Nelson.

The big dog took it gently, then lay down and began to gnaw it, his tail thumping enthusiastically on the floor.

Mr. Longbridge patted him. "It's strange," he said. "When you lose a dog, you think you'll never feel the same way about another one. But then, along comes a dog who seems really special. . . ."

Neil felt a surge of hope. Was Mr. Longbridge going to offer to take Nelson home with him?

Mr. Longbridge caught Neil's eye and smiled. "I've spoken to Mrs. Trimble about Nelson. She'd be glad for me to have him, as long as it's all right with your

father. I've also agreed to take Mr. Gilmour and Flash to the hydrotherapy pool once a week. I love to drive, and Nelson can go, too. Gentle exercise will be good for his diabetes."

Neil punched the air. Mr. Longbridge and Nelson would be great together, and Flash would improve now, too. "Let's go and tell everyone the good news!" he practically shouted.

Sarah was very quiet during Christmas lunch. "Are you not feeling well?" asked Bob, touching her forehead.

Sarah shrugged. "I'm not hungry." *She looks pale,* Neil thought.

Emily squeezed her arm. "But it's Christmas lunch. We only get it once a year!"

Sarah got down from the table and ran into the living room. Carole stood up to go after her.

"I'll go," Neil offered.

Sarah was lying on the couch with her knees drawn up and her head buried under a cushion.

Neil perched on the arm of the couch. "What's up, Squirt?"

Sarah began to cry.

Neil slid down beside her and put his arm around her. She clung to him, sobbing. "I keep thinking about Belle. I don't want Mom and Dad to give her away."

"Oh, Sarah," Neil said helplessly. He didn't know how to comfort her. He felt bad about having to give up Belle, too, but at least he had Jake. "Maybe somebody in town will adopt her," he said. "Then you'll still be able to see her."

"I don't want to see her with someone else," she cried. "I want her to stay with me. I love her and she loves me."

Neil stared at the lights on the tree. Suddenly, it didn't feel like Christmas anymore.

Carole came into the room carrying two presents wrapped in shiny blue paper and decorated with silver bows. Emily, Mr. Longbridge, and Jake were with her. "Your dad and I thought we'd give you your main presents now," she said. "We can have our Christmas pudding afterward."

Mr. Longbridge sat down in a chair near the fire. Emily sat on the hearth rug. Jake padded over and flopped down with his head on Neil's feet.

"Where's Dad?" Neil asked.

"He had to go and get something," replied Carole. "He'll be here in a minute." She sat beside Sarah and patted her shoulder. Sarah sat up and Carole handed her a tissue. "Are you all right now?"

Sarah nodded, then blew her nose.

Bob came into the room, shutting the door firmly behind him. He nodded to Carole.

"Here you are," said Carole. She handed Neil the smaller of the two presents, then gave the other to Emily.

"Thanks," Neil said.

"Can we open them now?" asked Emily.

"Definitely," said Carole. She stroked Sarah's hair. "You'll have to wait a minute for your present, sweetie pie."

Neil tore open his present to reveal a neat cardboard box. "Wow! A stopwatch for timing Jake's agility practice!" he exclaimed. "Cool!" He opened the box and took out the impressive-looking watch. "Yes! It's even got memory, so I'll be able to save and compare runs."

Emily opened her present more slowly. It was a photo album. "What's this?" she asked, puzzled.

"Look inside," said Carole.

Emily opened the album and her face lit up. "Photos of Saba!" She beamed at Carole and Bob. "This is amazing!"

"Who's Saba?" asked Mr. Longbridge.

"My leopard," Emily explained. "He lives in an African safari park and I've adopted him."

As Emily started to leaf through the album, Neil heard bells jingling. The sound seemed to be coming from the hallway. "What's that?" he asked.

Sarah looked up. "Is it Santa Claus?"

"It's something even better," said Bob, grinning. He opened the door and a tiny dark shape hurtled into the room. It was Belle! She was wearing her collar of jingle bells.

"Merry Christmas, Sarah!" said Carole. "Belle is *your* Christmas present."

"Belle!" Sarah shrieked. She threw herself on the puppy, hugging her, while Belle licked her wildly.

Bob beamed down at them. "Your mom and I thought we'd make an exception, just this once, and hold on to the little pup. You've looked after her very well, Sarah, and she certainly seems to get along with Jake."

Neil grinned at Emily. "What a great Christmas! Nelson's found a good home, Belle's staying at King Street, and the play was a huge success."

"*And* we'll be able to go sledding," Emily reminded

him. "We should take the sled up to the park first thing tomorrow morning."

"Let's not worry about tomorrow," said Bob. "There's some delicious Christmas pudding getting cold in the kitchen. I don't know about you, but I think we should go and eat it!"